Doggie
in the Window

Groundwood Books / Douglas & McIntyre
720 Bathurst Street, Suite 500, Toronto, Ontario M5S 2R4
Distributed in the USA by Publishers Group West
1700 Fourth Street, Berkeley, CA 94710

We acknowledge for their financial support of our publishing program the
Canada Council for the Arts, the Government of Canada through the Book
Publishing Industry Development Program (BPIDP), the Ontario Arts Council
and the Government of Ontario through the Ontario Media Development
Corporation's Ontario Book Initiative.

ONTARIO ARTS COUNCIL
CONSEIL DES ARTS DE L'ONTARIO

National Library of Canada Cataloguing in Publication
Arsenault, Elaine
Doggie in the window / by Elaine Arsenault ; illustrated by Fanny.
ISBN 0-88899-619-5
I. Fanny II. Title.
PS8551.R8277D63 2004   jC813'.6   C2004-900974-5

Printed and bound in China

*To my sister Madeleine, her husband, Rainer,
and their three muses, Adelaide, Amelia and
Willem, who believe in all dreams, even those of
little dogs…*

*Special thanks to Barbara Creary who, with her
love of good stories, always encouraged me to
write, and also to Steven Alves, for his
mischievousness and his patience.*

Elaine

*To my friend Manon and to her little
companions Chatouille, Titi, Frimousse
and Atchoum.*

Fanny

Doggie
in the Window

Elaine Arsenault

Pictures by

Fanny

A GROUNDWOOD BOOK

DOUGLAS & McINTYRE

TORONTO   VANCOUVER   BERKELEY

Monsieur Albert was sitting at the counter of his pet store reading the morning paper. He could see Mademoiselle Madeleine as she hurried around the corner. Ribbons floated from her coat and colored buttons spilled from her pockets as she rushed toward her costume shop next door.

She didn't seem to notice Doggie who was, as usual, sitting in the window.

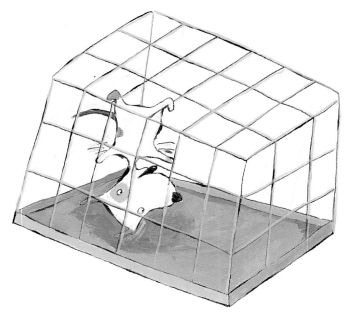

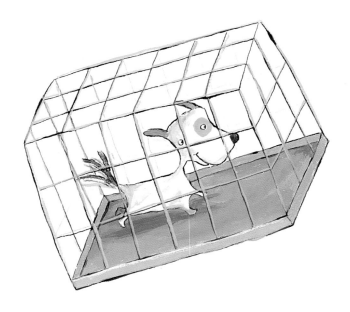

Doggie dreamed of being adopted by Mademoiselle Madeleine. But no matter how cute Doggie was, how adorably he behaved, no matter how enthusiastically he wagged his tail, she didn't seem to notice him.

That night Monsieur Albert locked up and went home. The store was quiet as the light from the street lamp streamed through the window. All the pets but one were fast asleep. Doggie was wide awake, wondering why Mademoiselle Madeleine never noticed him, when he saw that the latch on his cage was undone.

Doggie jumped onto the floor. He was playing with his tail when he noticed a light coming through a hole in the wall. Peering through the hole, he saw Mademoiselle Madeleine hard at work at her sewing machine. She was pulling threads, folding ribbons, nipping and tucking fabric. Snippets of cloth flew here, there and everywhere.

Doggie had never seen anything so lovely.

When Mademoiselle Madeleine had finished she got up, plunked her hat on her head, put on her gloves and walked out.

One day I'll be a seamstress just like her, thought Doggie.

He squeezed through the hole into the shop. Fabric, felt and feathers lay on the floor. The walls were lined with rolls of tiger and zebra prints. Next to the machine was a wooden box filled with thread in all the colors of the rainbow.

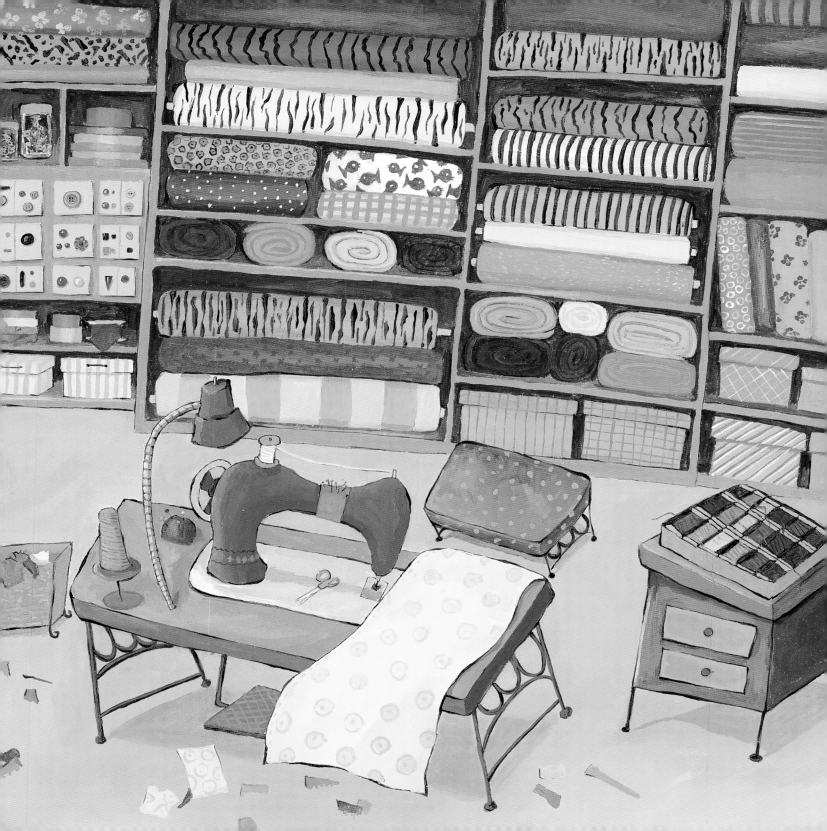

Doggie had an idea. He knew how to make Mademoiselle Madeleine notice him. He got to work.

All night he toiled — cutting, pinning and snipping.

He pressed seams,
stitched ribbons and sewed
on buttons until dawn.

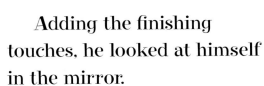

Adding the finishing
touches, he looked at himself
in the mirror.
Well done, he thought. I
look gorgeous!

The brass bell over the door tinkled as Monsieur
Albert walked into the shop.

Something's different, he thought.

Doggie sat among the kittens. He was wearing a
zebra-print kitten costume. His kitten bonnet was tied
under his chin, and his pipe-cleaner whiskers wobbled.
His thin cat's tail wagged.

Mademoiselle Madeleine rushed by. She saw Doggie,
tapped on the window and called out to Monsieur
Albert, "What an odd-looking kitten you've got there."
She noticed me, thought Doggie.
"You are not like other dogs," said Monsieur Albert.

That night when Mademoiselle Madeleine had put on her hat and gloves and walked out, Doggie slipped into the shop. He pulled stretchy fabric this way and that. He tied multi-colored ribbons to his tail. In a drawer he found a perfect bathing cap.

"Amazing!" he exclaimed when he was finished.

The next morning Doggie sucked in his belly and squeezed into his goldfish suit. As soon as he saw a green shoe coming around the corner, he dove into the aquarium.

Water splashed over the rim as Doggie paddled and dove. The fish darted behind the plants.

Mademoiselle Madeleine rapped on the window, and Monsieur Albert looked up from his paper.

"I think your fish needs water wings," she said and walked away.

She noticed me, Doggie thought, as Monsieur Albert pulled him dripping out of the tank.

Doggie was hugely encouraged.

That night he gathered up all the feathers that had fallen to Mademoiselle Madeleine's floor.

When she came around the corner the next day, she wasn't rushing as usual. Doggie was perched on the birdcage swing, balancing on one leg next to the parrot. His suit was made of turquoise feathers, and he had an orange beak over his nose. As Mademoiselle Madeleine leaned over for a closer look, Doggie wagged his tail and knocked the parrot off the perch. Birdseed and feathers flew through the air.

What an odd bird, thought Mademoiselle Madeleine.

The next morning Monsieur Albert found Doggie clinging to the wall. Green suction cups were fastened to his paws. He was dressed as a lizard.

Monsieur Albert detached Doggie from the wall and carried him under his arm. As he passed the counter, Doggie's paws stuck to the cash register and knocked over the dog treats and fish food that were standing there.

As he was helping Doggie out of his costume, Monsieur Albert heard the bell tinkle.

It was Mademoiselle Madeleine.

Doggie's heart beat fast with hope.
Mademoiselle Madeleine looked into his
brown eyes and said, "That's a fine doggie
you have there, but why on earth
is he dressed like a lizard?"

"He made this costume himself.
Doggie wants to be a seamstress just
like you," said Monsieur Albert.

"But I don't need another
seamstress," said Mademoiselle Madeleine.

Doggie's heart sank.

"But look at all the costumes he has made," said Monsieur Albert. "A cat costume, a bird costume, a fish costume, as well as the lizard!"

"I don't want a seamstress," said Mademoiselle Madeleine, "but I can certainly use a costume designer. He's just what I need!"

Doggie's tail wagged so hard he knocked all the packages of fish food off the shelf.

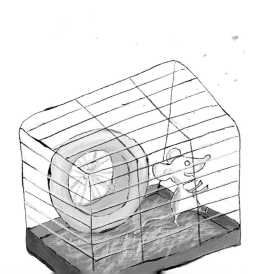

Now every morning Monsieur Albert sees Mademoiselle Madeleine
and Doggie hurrying by his window on the way to the costume shop.
Ribbons float from Doggie's coat and colored buttons spill out of his
pockets.

Even a small dog can have a big dream. And make it come true.